For Niki, who knew how to play
C. L. S.
To Alain Corbel
P. P.

First edition 2008

Library of Congress Cataloging-in-Publication Data is available.
Library of Congress Catalog Card Number 2007052024
ISBN 978-0-7636-2006-6

2 4 6 8 10 9 7 5 3 1

Printed in Singapore

This book was typeset in Kosmik.
The illustrations were done in acrylic on paper.

Candlewick Press
2067 Massachusetts Avenue
Cambridge, Massachusetts 02140

visit us at www.candlewick.com

BiG
Little Monkey

Carole Lexa Schaefer illustrated by Pierre Pratt

CANDLEWICK PRESS
CAMBRIDGE, MASSACHUSETTS

Early one morning,
in Big Mango Tree,
Little Monkey woke up
and looked around.

His whole family, with full tummies and drowsy heads, was still asleep—even Dear Mama.

"No more sleeping," chattered Little Monkey. "Time to play!"

He tickled their toes. He sang in their ears.

He tugged Dear Mama's tail. "Chee-chatta-chee.
Come play with me," he begged.

"Too early, Little Monkey," murmured Dear Mama.
"Wait awhile and be still."

Little Monkey tried to do as Dear Mama said.

But his tail twitched

and his feet itched until . . .

he decided, "Hey, I am a big little monkey now. I can go find someone else to play with."

And, hand over hand,
bim-ba-lah, bim-ba-lah,
Little Monkey swung away until . . .

he spied Steady Sloth resting
upside down in a cecropia tree.

"Good morning," called Little Monkey.

"Huh . . . huh . . . huh," said Steady Sloth
in her slow, quiet way. "And why is a little
monkey like you up and about so early?"

"I am a big little monkey now," said
Little Monkey. "And I would
like to play with you."

"Oh?" said Steady Sloth. "And what sort of thing can a frisky monkey play with a slow sloth?"

"I can play Hang Upside Down," said Little Monkey. "Just like you—see?" And, *bim-ba-lah*, he hung upside down beside her.

"*Just* like me?" said Steady Sloth. "Hush, then." And she closed her eyes to rest some more.

Uh-oh, thought Little Monkey, too quiet for me.

"Thank you, Steady Sloth," he said, and, *bim-ba-lah, bim-ba-lah*, he swung on until . . .

high in the trees, he came to the perch
of Proud Parrot, who was preening his feathers.

"Haloo, hello," chattered Little Monkey.

"*Rrr-ARK!*" cried the bird, looking at him with one
bright eye. "Why is a little monkey up so early
bothering me in the treetops?"

"I don't mean to bother you," said Little Monkey.
"I'm a big little monkey now, and I'd like to play
with you."

"Play?" croaked the bird. "Can you flip-flap your wings, then, and fly around and around in circles?"

"No," said Little Monkey. "But I can make up songs like you. Listen: *Chee-chatta-chee-chee, chatta-chatta-chee-chee.*"

"You think that sounds like ME?" screeched Proud Parrot. "Listen:

REE-awk,

WHEE-OO!

SQueee-SKWONK!

SKUH-GRACK,"

Oooh, too squawky for me, thought Little Monkey.

"See you later," he called, and, *bim-ba-lah, bim-ba-lah*, he swung along until . . .

low down in the trees, he found Sly Boa draped over many branches.

"Sssay there," hissed Sly Boa, "what's a little monkey doing all alone in my part of the foressst?"

In his biggest voice, Little Monkey said, "I am a big little monkey and I am playing Curl My Tail Around in Tricky Ways. Like you."

"Sssome sssay I am all tail," Sly Boa hissed softly. "Did you know?" He slithered closer—*riss-a-riss.*

Little Monkey was sure that Sly Boa was much more than tail. *Bim-ba-lah*—he flipped himself up to a higher branch.

"Clever little monkey," hissed the snake, and he slithered closer once more—*riss-a-riss.* "Will you breakfassst with me?"

Uh-oh, thought Little Monkey, *way too tricky for me.*

"No, thanks!" he hollered as—*bimbalah bimbalah*—faster than any boa's slither, he swung far away until . . .

he found himself back in the middle of Big Mango Tree.

Little Monkey looked around.

On the branches nearby sat his whole family—wide awake.

"Where were you, Little Monkey?" they chattered. "And what were you doing?"

"While you were sleeping," said Little Monkey, patting his chest, "I hung out with Sloth, sang for Parrot, and slipped away from Boa."

"*Boa!*" cried all the monkeys together.

"Yes, I'm a big little monkey now," said Little Monkey.
"But, *chee-chatta-chee*, I can also stay here and play
with you."

Dear Mama cocked her head. "And why would a
big little monkey want to do that?"

Bim-ba-lah—he swung up beside her. "Because, Dear Mama, sometimes I am still your Little Monkey, too."